Dreamland

Rohini Priya & Asma

Ukiyoto Publishing

All global publishing rights are held by

Ukiyoto Publishing

Published in 2023

Content Copyright © Rohini Priya

ISBN 9789360165857

All rights reserved.

No part of this publication may be reproduced, transmitted, or stored in a retrieval system, in any form by any means, electronic, mechanical, photocopying, recording or otherwise, without the prior permission of the publisher.

The moral rights of the author have been asserted.

This is a work of fiction. Names, characters, businesses, places, events, locales, and incidents are either the products of the author's imagination or used in a fictitious manner. Any resemblance to actual persons, living or dead, or actual events is purely coincidental.

This book is sold subject to the condition that it shall not by way of trade or otherwise, be lent, resold, hired out or otherwise circulated, without the publisher's prior consent, in any form of binding or cover other than that in which it is published.

This title is produced in Association with Pachyderm Tales

www.pachydermtales.com

ACKNOWLEDGEMENT

I whole heartedly thank,

Mohanasundari Jaganathan,

(Managing Director of Sharp Electrodes Pvt Ltd)

for funding this project.

Without her, this book would not be possible!

This book was a part of workshop conducted in our college, NGM College Pollachi and Pachyderm Tales.

I whole heartedly thank our management, our teachers and HOD of English Dept, NGM as well as Suja Mam for this initiative.

Thanks to my friend to support and help me to complete my work.

Dreamland 1

A cute little baby was lying on a bed, sleeping like a cat. Her name is Sufi. She dreamed about something while she was asleep.

In that dream, Sufi saw a forest and a huge palace in it.

"Is anybody here?" she shouted.

As Sufi walked, she noticed many flowers, animals, and birds all around her and started playing with them.

Dreamland 3

While she was playing, Sufi was suddenly visited by an angel.

Sufi was shocked when she saw the angel and dropped the flowers she was holding to the ground.

The angel and Sufi started conversing.

Sufi asked the angel, "*Who are you?*"

The angel replied, "*I am the Angel of the forest.*"

"*Flowers, birds, animals and all that is here are my friends. However, there is a lady who wants to capture me and my palace.*

She wants to destroy the forest. Others called her the Devil. She has a black cat with her, wore a black dress, and wore a black hat." replied the Angel, imagining the woman's picture in her mind.

Dreamland 5

"*I would like to see that Devil. Will you call me and take me to meet her?*" inquired Sufi, surprisingly.

"*Meeting her is dangerous.*" warned the Angel.

Later, they held hands and walked by the lake as the angel spoke about the secret book in the palace.

Dreamland 7

Suddenly, Sufi and Angel heard a sound and tried to figure out where it came from. To their surprise, they saw the Devil flying over the lake and she flew down back to them.

Sufi was frightened and hid behind the Angel's gown. A dark thought takes up the devil's mind.

Dreamland 9

"If I could manage to seize the girl away, I could make the Angel surrender before me. Alas! Then there will be no one to rule. I will be the king of this forest.", she thought to herself.

Her evilness provoked the Angel to wage a war against the Devil.

They started flicking their magic wands. The Devil abducts Sufi in between the fight and flies high and far away, taking Sufi with her.

The Angel followed them.

Dreamland 11

As they reached the Devils's hut,

Devil notices that the Angel has followed them and starts another fight.

The Angel, who was not interested in violence, requested the Devil to leave the little girl alone and safe.

"If you need the girl that badly, surrender all your powers, palace, wealth, and all that you own in front of me.

Think…think about it all and answer. If you refuse to do so, the girl will spend the rest of her life as my slave." saying this, the devil laughs loudly "Ha Ha Ha"

Without any further thought, the angel agreed to the devil's demands and decided to give away all her belongings and powers to the devil.

The devil was astonished and was jittery with excitement and happiness. She laughed out loud.

As the devil sucks up all the power from the angel's body, the angel falls down, dead. Sufi left abandoned and sad.

She tries to wake up the angel while crying and kisses the angel.

.

.

.

All her efforts were in vain.

Suddenly, she thinks about the secret book in the palace.

Sufi ran to the palace, taking all her strength and wit to not get caught by the Devil who was still following her.

The devil rushes behind little Sufi to kill her. She enters the palace and hides behind a huge pillar so as to cover herself from the sight of the devil.

Sufi waits for the Devil to leave and finally comes out and searches for the secret room. She finds a room in the corner enclosed by a giant door.

Taking out all her strength, Sufi pushed the wooden door, opening it.

She stepped inside the room and found the secret book that contained all the magical tricks and chantings.

She read them all and tried remembering some of the powerful chantings to use against the devil. Sufi tried chanting it numerous times, but it didn't show any effect at all.

Dreamland 19

Finally, she imagined the smiling face of the Angel in her mind and tried chanting one last time.

And there it goes, destructing the wooden door in to millions of pieces.

Dreamland 21

Hearing the huge thud, the Devil appears in front of Sufi. She pointed her magic wand towards the little Sufi and murmured something.

The lightning produced from the wand made Sufi fall with a thud. She got up, memorized the chanting, and spelt it with zeal and confidence.

The unexpected act by Sufi let the devil fall on to the ground, breaking her ribs. All her attempts to get up were unsuccessful.

Sufi chanted yet another spell and the devil was dead. Soon as the soul left her body, the angelic powers started getting transmitted back to the Angel.

Dreamland 23

The Angel regained her consciousness and woke up to see the dead devil. Sufi ran to her and hugged her tightly. The angel kissed Sufi's cheek.

"Thank you, Sufi. You did a great job. You succeeded in defeating the Devil who was a threat to the forest.", said the Angel.

They held their hands again and walked deep in to the forest, talking to the trees and animals.

Dreamland

Suddenly, Sufi wakes up and sees no one around. She rubs her eyes and calls her mom to talk about the dream.

Mom asked Sufi, "*What have you learnt from your dream?*"

Sufi tells her mom, "*We should only do and think about good things. If our thoughts are wicked, it will lead to our own disaster.*"

Sufi's mom kissed her on the forehead and smiled.

The Author

Rohini Priya. D is an English literature final year student at NGM college Pollachi. She is an innovative writer, and artist. Her story, "The Dream Land" shows her love for writing, especially in the genres of fantasy, and magic. She wishes to be a children's writer and lay out new dimensions for storytelling. Her primary motive is to deliver happiness to her readers and to cheer them through the innocence of children, embedded in her writing.

The Illustrator

Asma is an English literature student of NGM college. She is an innovative artist, writer, and illustrator, who loves fantasy. Dahlia is her first book; through Dahlia she is trying spread happiness and power a smile. This is her second book as an illustrator.

www.ingramcontent.com/pod-product-compliance
Lightning Source LLC
LaVergne TN
LVHW041643070526
838199LV00053B/3531